Silvermane
Saves the Stars

Daisy Meadows

ORCHARD

To Annabel Brady

Special thanks to Conrad Mason

ORCHARD BOOKS

First published in Great Britain in 2020 by The Watts Publishing Group

1 3 5 7 9 10 8 6 4 2

Text copyright © 2020 Working Partners Limited
Illustrations © Orchard Books 2020
Series created by Working Partners Limited

A CIP catalogue record for this book is available from the British Library.

ISBN 978 1 40835 700 2

Printed and bound in Great Britain by Clays Ltd, Elcograf S.p.A.

The paper and board used in this book are made from wood from responsible sources.

Orchard Books
An imprint of Hachette Children's Group
Part of The Watts Publishing Group Limited
Carmelite House
50 Victoria Embankment
London EC4Y 0DZ

An Hachette UK Company
www.hachette.co.uk
www.hachettechildrens.co.uk

Contents

Aisha and Emily are best friends from Spellford Village. Aisha loves sports, whilst Emily's favourite thing is science. But what both girls enjoy more than anything is visiting Enchanted Valley and helping their unicorn friends, who live there.

Silvermane

Silvermane and the other Night Sparkle Unicorns make sure night-time is magical. Silvermane's locket helps her take care of the stars.

Dreamspell's magic brings sweet dreams to all the creatures of Enchanted Valley. Without her magical powers, everyone will have nightmares!

Dreamspell

With the help of her magical friends and the power of her locket, Slumbertail makes sure everyone in Enchanted Valley has a peaceful night's sleep.

Slumbertail

Kindly Brighteye is in charge of the moon. The magic of her locket helps its beautiful light to shine each night.

Brighteye

Enchanted Cottage

Golden Palace

An Enchanted Valley lies a twinkle away,
Where beautiful unicorns live, laugh and play
You can visit the mermaids, or go for a ride,
So much fun to be had, but dangers can hide!

Your friends need your help – this is how you know:
A keyring lights up with a magical glow.
Whirled off like a dream, you won't want to leave.
Friendship forever, when you truly believe.

Chapter One
A Unicorn Made of Stars

Emily Turner gazed around in wonder. "Your garden looks even more magical at twilight!" she said.

Her best friend, Aisha Khan, grinned and spread a tartan blanket on the grass.

The moon shone like a new coin, and in the middle of the lawn, the stone statue

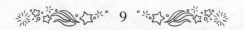

of a phoenix gleamed against the deep blue sky. It looked as though it might take off at any moment.

"That's because of all this starlight!" said Aisha.

The girls lay next to each other on the blanket, staring upwards. The air was chilly, and they snuggled up to each other to stay warm. As their eyes got used to the dark, Emily and Aisha saw the stars glitter like silver pinpricks in a dark blue curtain.

"Wow ..." breathed Emily.

"I'm so glad my parents let you stay over," said Aisha happily.

"And not just for one night," said Emily. "A whole week of sleepovers! It's going to be brilliant." She gasped. "Hey, I can see the Big Dipper!" Emily pointed to a small pattern of stars, shaped a bit like a wheelbarrow. "The stars always come out in patterns, which are called constellations. I've been reading about them. The Big Dipper is part of Ursa Major. Then there's Aquarius, Scorpio …"

"What about that one?" said Aisha. She pointed to a group of stars that suddenly began to shine brighter than all the others.

Emily frowned. "I don't know … It's not in my book. It looks almost like …"

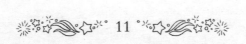

"A unicorn!" said both girls, at the same time.

They sat up and looked at each other, eyes wide. They were thinking of Enchanted Valley, a secret land they had visited together, where unicorns lived with lots of other magical creatures.

Emily reached into her pocket and drew out the glass unicorn keyring that Aurora, Queen of Enchanted Valley, had given the girls so she could summon them back. To her delight, it was shimmering with multi-coloured lights. "Queen Aurora is calling us again!"

Aisha pulled out her own keyring. It was sparkling too, just like Emily's.

The girls knew what to do. They gently

touched the tips of the unicorn horns against each other. At once there was a whooshing sound and a burst of light, like a firework going off. Colourful sparks showered all around. Then the girls felt themselves rising into the air. Their feet left the blanket and they hovered.

"We're going back to Enchanted Valley!" squealed Aisha. She and Emily held hands tightly.

A haze of light glimmered all around.

Then slowly they began to drift down,
until they landed on a patch of grass.

They weren't in Emily's garden any
more. Instead they stood at the bottom of
a gentle hill. Up the slope was an elegant
golden palace with turrets shaped like
unicorn horns, silhouetted against the
purple sky.

"It's twilight in Enchanted Valley, too!"

said Aisha. "Wow!
Isn't it beautiful?"

"Let's go and see
Queen Aurora,"
said Emily. "I bet
she's waiting for us
at the palace!"

As the girls

climbed the hill, the sky turned a deeper purple, and shadows crept across the fields and woodland on every side.

They had nearly reached the moat that surrounded the palace, when the drawbridge began to swing downwards. Its silver chains rattled as it fell with a soft thump across the water. But to the girls' surprise, it wasn't Queen Aurora who came trotting out. Instead, four unicorns appeared, their hooves clip-clopping on the drawbridge. The first was the silvery colour of the stars, with a blue mane and tail with silver highlights. She was followed by a lilac unicorn wearing a silver saddlebag, then a very pale pink unicorn with a beautiful pink mane and

tail, and finally a pale blue one with a
gorgeous blue mane. Like all unicorns in
Enchanted Valley, every one of them wore
a delicate silver locket around their neck.

"Do you think they'll know where
Aurora is?" whispered Aisha.

Before Emily could reply, the four
unicorns formed a little circle on the

grass, then slowly lowered their heads until the tips of their horns touched.

A soft chime rang out, like the sound of a little bell. The four horns began to glow, and the girls saw that the unicorns' lockets were glowing too. *Magic!*

As the chime died away, night fell completely across Enchanted Valley. For a moment the glow from the unicorns was the only light in the darkness. Then Emily gasped and pointed up into the sky.

The stars were coming out, blinking into life like a sprinkling of magic dust. The whole valley glittered with a beautiful white light.

"It's incredible," gasped Aisha, gazing out over the fields and the forest.

Everything looked as though it had been
made from silver.

"I'm so glad we get to visit at night-
time," said Emily.

Just then, the silver unicorn turned
and blinked at them. "Oh my," she said,
flicking her tail. "You must be Emily and
Aisha. Welcome!"

Chapter Two
Night Sparkle

"We've heard so much about you!" gushed the pink unicorn.

"You stood up to Selena when she stole the lockets from the Nature Unicorns!" added the lilac unicorn with the saddlebag. "Oh, it's so good to meet you!"

"We're the Night Sparkle Unicorns,"

said the blue unicorn, proudly lifting her head. "We bring night-time to Enchanted Valley."

"Hello!" said the girls.

"I'm Silvermane," said the last unicorn. Sure enough, her mane and tail had highlights as silver as her coat. "My locket gives me the magic I need to take care of the stars."

The girls peered closer at the little glass locket. Inside, they saw a golden gleam. It was a tiny shooting star, its tail sparkling behind it.

"It's beautiful," gasped Aisha.

"I'm Dreamspell," said the lilac unicorn. "I make sure everyone in the valley has nice dreams. Slumbertail here helps everyone sleep peacefully." The pink unicorn tossed her tail, looking bashful. "And Brighteye is in charge of the moon." The blue unicorn bowed her head.

"It's so nice to meet you all!" said Emily and Aisha together.

The girls admired the unicorns' lockets.
Slumbertail's had a tiny, fluffy white
pillow floating inside it. Brighteye's was a
little golden sliver – a crescent moon.

Dreamspell's locket was the strangest
of the four. As Emily and Aisha watched,
it changed from a little group of friends
having a picnic, to a sunny seaside scene,
and then to a birthday party.

"Oh, it's just like a lovely dream!" said

Emily with a happy sigh.

"Is Queen Aurora here, too?" asked Aisha. "We thought she summoned us."

"I hope Selena isn't causing trouble again," said Emily anxiously.

The girls exchanged a glance. Every time they had visited Enchanted Valley, the wicked unicorn Selena had been trying to force the other unicorns to make her queen by stealing their magical lockets.

Slumbertail gave a little shiver, her big eyes wide. "She's so mean and scary!"

"We haven't seen Selena since the last time you were here," said Silvermane. "But we know where Queen Aurora is."

"Actually, we were just about to go to

Shimmer Bay to meet her," explained Brighteye. "When she left she said she'd be back today. That must be why she summoned you, because her ship is on its way home."

"Her ship?" asked Aisha.

"A few days ago, we found a message in a bottle, washed up on the beach," Dreamspell explained. "It was from someone called Aneles, and it was asking for help! So Queen Aurora went to find this Aneles."

"We're bringing Aurora some hot cocoa to welcome her home," said Slumbertail. She nodded at the little saddlebag that Dreamspell was wearing. "And a warm, fluffy blanket. She'll be

tired when she gets back!"

The girls' hearts fizzed with excitement at the thought of seeing Queen Aurora's ship come sailing into Shimmer Bay. "Can we come too?" asked Aisha.

"Of course!" said Brighteye.

They all set off down the hillside. In the distance they could just see the ocean beyond the treetops. The waves sparkled like diamonds in the moonlight.

When they reached the bottom of the hill, the Night Sparkle Unicorns led the way through a shadowy forest. Their horns glowed softly, bobbing up and down like fireflies as they walked.

At last they emerged from the forest, and the girls saw a smooth, sandy beach

up ahead, curving in a shimmering
crescent around the bay.

"Wow!" gasped Emily. "It looks so
beautiful at night!"

On the beach, families of animals were
heading home after a day of playing. A
group of young rabbits shook out their
beach towels and rolled them up. A family
of pixies were packing up their buckets

and spades, their wings glinting in the light of the stars. Overhead, bats wheeled, squeaking happily to each other.

"The bats aren't going to bed. They're nocturnal animals!" said Emily. "That means they come out at night-time, and sleep during the day."

"Hey," said Aisha, pointing at one of the bats. "Isn't that Flit?"

Sure enough, the plump little bat flapped over to them, squawking cheerfully. "Hello, girls!"

"Hello, Flit!" called Emily and Aisha, waving. The bat had been Selena's servant, but after he realised how mean she was, he had helped Emily and Aisha to stop her horrible plans.

The girls' feet sank deep in the soft sand, as they followed the Night Sparkle Unicorns across the dunes. A breeze ruffled their clothes, and they could hear the waves lapping gently at the shore.

"We should have brought a bucket and spade!" said Emily with a grin.

Just then, the girls noticed a glittering golden creature swooping among the bats. It glided down and landed on the beach not far away, folding its wings neatly. It had a long, sweeping tail, shining black eyes and a silver beak. Every one of its feathers looked like it was made from pure gold.

"It's Lumi the Lightingale," said Slumbertail, as the bird hopped across the sand towards them.

Emily frowned. "Do you mean *nightingale*?"

Silvermane laughed delightedly. "No! Show them, Lumi."

Lumi spread his wings and closed his
eyes. All at once, his golden feathers
began to glow, as though they were on
fire. They shone brighter and brighter,
lighting up the whole beach until the girls
had to look away.

"That's amazing, Lumi!" said Aisha.

Lumi's light faded, and he blinked
several times. "Wow, that was really

bright," he chirped, still squinting. "I mean … thank you!"

The girls laughed. The lightingale seemed amazed by his own magic!

"Lumi is the keeper of the Starlight House," Silvermane explained. Using her horn, she pointed to a high, rugged cliff at the far end of the bay. The girls saw a tall white tower on top of it, surrounded by craggy rocks. A silvery beam shone from its topmost window.

"It's a special lamp," said Silvermane, "powered by starlight. Lumi uses it to show where the rocks are, so that ships can sail safely to the beach." She lowered her hoof, frowning. "But what are you doing here, Lumi? Queen Aurora's ship should be arriving any minute."

Lumi swished a wing impatiently. "Oh, don't worry about that. I've got something much more important to do." With a squawk he surged up into the air and began to fly in circles round and round the Night Sparkle Unicorns, furiously flapping his wings.

Emily and Aisha frowned at each other. They were both thinking the same thing. *Something's not right …*

"Look!" cried Emily suddenly. Purple smoke had swirled up from the sand, coiling round the unicorns. Silvermane and the others shuffled closer to each other, tossing their manes anxiously. Emily and Aisha couldn't help huddling

with them too.

"What's happening?" wailed
Dreamspell.

"It's some sort of magic spell!" said
Brighteye.

The smoke got thicker and thicker, until
the girls couldn't see the unicorns at all.
Then – *whoosh!* – the smoke evaporated.
The unicorns looked around, puzzled.

Aisha gasped. "Your lockets! They're
gone!"

Lumi was still flying in circles above
their heads. But now the lightingale had
four shining objects dangling on chains
from his beak.

"And Lumi's stolen them!" cried Emily.

Chapter Three
Endless Night

One by one, the unicorns' horns stopped glowing. The stars winked out. A deep darkness fell across the beach, until the only light was the silvery beam from the Starlight House. Then, at last, that flickered and died too.

The animals all around squeaked and

squealed with dismay.

Emily and Aisha held hands. "I can hardly see a thing!" said Emily, peering at the shadowy shapes across the sand.

"Lumi, come back!" Aisha called into the darkness.

There was no reply.

"I can't believe Lumi stole our lockets!" cried Silvermane from nearby. "What's got into him?"

Emily and Aisha stared up into the sky, but they couldn't see the lightingale.

"Oh no!" said Aisha, clapping a hand over her mouth. "I've just realised … Without the Starlight House, Queen Aurora's ship won't be able to sail safely to the shore."

"She'll be stuck out at sea," said Emily. "Or worse — she'll hit a rock!"

The animals were still wailing with distress, and the girls heard scuffs and thumps as even the foxes and porcupines — who could normally see well at night — blundered into each other in the dark.

"We have to stick together," said Aisha, with determination. She squeezed Emily's hand tightly. "Hey, don't you think it's strange that Lumi stole the lockets just when Queen Aurora needs the light to get home from helping Aneles?"

Emily frowned. "Hang on a second. *Aneles* …" She quickly found a bit of driftwood. She traced out the letters of the name in the sand, kneeling down and squinting to see.

The girls both gasped at the same time.

"Uh-oh," breathed Aisha. "Aneles spelled backwards is … Selena!"

"She must have written the note to trick Aurora!" cried Silvermane.

"And it worked, of course!" said a triumphant voice.

Everyone looked around nervously. "Who was th-that?" stammered Dreamspell.

The whole bay suddenly lit up with a white flash of lightning. Then thunder rolled in the distance. *BOOM!* A silver unicorn came leaping from the sky, her purple mane and tail fluttering as she swooped down. Her hooves hit the beach with a thud, sending up a spray of sand.

The girls stared in horror. *Selena!*

Just then, a golden bird came fluttering from Selena's shoulders. It was Lumi, still clutching the lockets in his beak. The lightingale beat his wings. Then, with a *POP* and a puff of purple smoke, his tail grew shorter, his feathers turned brown

and his eyes became huge.

"He's not a lightingale at all!" gasped
Emily. "He's an owl!"

"And I fooled you all with my magical
disguise!" scoffed the little owl. "Ha ha!
I'm too clever for you!" He puffed his
chest out proudly.

"Quiet, Screech!" roared Selena. "It
was my plan, so I'm the clever one!" She
tossed her mane and drew herself up. "I'm
going to keep all your lockets, and this

horrible dark night is going to last for
ever …"

"We won't let that happen," said Emily,
stepping forward bravely.

"The only way to stop me is to make
me Queen of Enchanted Valley!" Selena
cried.

"No way!" said Aisha. "Aurora is the
true queen!"

"You might just change your mind
when you see how miserable Enchanted
Valley will become," sneered Selena.
"I hope you aren't scared of the dark!"
She cackled, and Screech sniggered
along. "Now if you'll excuse me," said
Selena, "I'm off to hide the star locket in
the darkest, most dangerous place in the

whole valley! You'll never be able to get it back, and Aurora will never get back to shore safely!"

Still cackling, Selena rose into the air. Lightning flashed again, and thunder rolled in the distance as she soared through the sky with Screech flapping along behind her.

When the lightning faded, the wicked unicorn was gone, and the beach was left in darkness.

"Oh no," whispered Silvermane in a small voice. "What are we going to do? Without the lockets we can't look after night-time in Enchanted Valley."

"And the night will never end!" wailed Dreamspell.

"And Aurora will be in danger!" said Brighteye, bowing her head.

"Unless we make Selena queen," sniffed Slumbertail.

The girls held hands tighter than ever. They knew just what the other was thinking. *We can't let that happen!*

"Don't worry," said Emily firmly.

"We'll stop Selena."

"We're going to find those lockets," said Aisha. "And save Enchanted Valley!"

Chapter Four
Go Glow Potion

"First things first," said Emily. "We need to find the star locket, so that the stars will come out again, and the Starlight House will work properly. Then Queen Aurora can get home safely."

"And we have to find the real Lumi!" added Aisha. "I hope he's all right, wherever he is."

"I'll come with you," said Silvermane, tossing back her mane. "After all, it's my locket." Then she sighed heavily. "But how are we going to find the locket without any light?"

Aisha snapped her fingers. "I know! Let's ask Hob. He's always mixing up magical potions … I bet he could make some light for us."

"Great idea," said Emily. Their goblin friend had helped them out many times before. "And I think I know who can guide us to his cottage." She put two fingers in her mouth and blew a piercing whistle. "Flit! Where are you, Flit?"

There was a rustle of leathery wings.

Then a small, shadowy shape came gliding down to land beside them on the beach. "Is Selena still here?" said Flit, his voice trembling.

"Don't worry," said Aisha. "She's gone. But do you think you could help us find Silvermane's locket to end all this darkness?"

"Well, I actually love the dark," Flit mumbled. Then he shook his wings, rustling them again. "But that doesn't matter. Selena is trying to ruin Enchanted Valley for everyone! I'll help you stop her."

"Thank you, Flit!" said Emily, grinning. "I was hoping you could guide us to Hob's cottage. Since you're a bat and use sound instead of light to find your way around, you're the best person to get us there in the dark."

"I certainly am!" said Flit, his eyes gleaming with pride. "Follow my voice!"

"I'll carry you girls," said Silvermane, as the little bat flapped up in the air.

Aisha clung on to Silvermane's neck, while Emily held tightly on to Aisha.

"Ready?" called Silvermane. "Then off we go!"

Flit began to sing:

**"Some might say I'm a funny little bat
But that's OK, I'm fine with that."**

The girls giggled as they listened to Flit's silly song.

**"I've got my friends and that's all I need
Selena won't win, she'll never succeed."**

The girls could feel themselves soaring up into the night sky, circling high above the beach, but they could hardly see a thing in the darkness. Their eyes watered, and their hair tangled in the wind. The unicorn's mane fluttered as they flew, tickling Aisha's face.

"This way!" cried Flit, flying low over the forest. "Watch out – big tree on the left! Oops – flying squirrels on the right!"

Silvermane followed close behind.

The girls kept blinking and staring, hoping their eyes would get used to the dark … but there was just blackness all around.

It felt as though they were flying for ages. But at long last, they heard Flit call out up ahead: "Time to land!" Then their stomachs lurched as Silvermane dipped downwards.

With a soft thump, the unicorn's hooves touched down. A short distance away they could just make out the familiar shape of a crooked old oak tree. They

heard the
creak of a door
opening, and
a little person
stepped out of
the tree trunk, a
glowing yellow
lantern dangling

from his hand. The girls felt a rush of
relief at being able to see light again.

"Hob!" cried Emily. The girls ran
forward and embraced the little goblin
tightly.

When they stepped away, Hob's
wrinkled green face had broken into a
huge smile. He adjusted his pointy hat
and pushed his spectacles back up his

nose. "My
goodness, it's
wonderful to
see you two!"
he squeaked.
"And dear old
Silvermane
too ... and little
Flit! Come in,
all of you!"

Hob kept
chattering
away as he

led them into the tree trunk and down a set of winding wooden steps. "Don't tell me … This horrible darkness is Selena's doing, isn't it? What a wicked unicorn! Dear me …"

They reached the bottom and stepped at last into Hob's underground cavern home. It was large, bright and cosy, with candles and lanterns glimmering on ledges across the rocky walls. The light flickered on a thousand dusty old bottles and boxes. The girls knew that every one was full of magical ingredients.

"You're right, Hob. And we were hoping you might be able to help us," said Emily.

"We really need some light," added Aisha. "So we can find Silvermane's magical locket and put a stop to Selena's plans."

"Of course!" said Hob, rubbing his hands together. "Don't worry, I've got just the thing. Even better than my old lantern! We'll mix up one of my extra-special Go Glow potions. Now, quickly, girls … I need a pinch of Bright Blossoms, a cup of Sunshine Dew and plenty of Fire Moss!"

Hob began to stir his big black cauldron, while Emily and Aisha hurried to find the ingredients from the shelves.

Flit hung upside down from a coat hook to watch as Emily tipped in the shining pink Bright Blossoms and the glowing yellow Sunshine Dew. Then Aisha heaved in an armful of prickly orange Fire Moss.

The mixture bubbled and spat, as Hob stirred it with a huge wooden spoon.

"Is it ready?" asked Silvermane, staring into the cauldron with wide eyes.

"It is now!" said Hob, sprinkling in a final handful of silver dust. He unhooked a small lantern made of metal and glass from the rocky ceiling and ladled the potion into its container. The liquid was bright orange and glowed like lava. "Time to test it," said Hob. "Shall we?"

They went outside and Aisha took the lantern from Hob. She opened its little metal door.

At once, the whole hillside was flooded with bright light. Emily and Aisha grinned. They could see every blade of grass, as clear as day.

"It's perfect!" cried Emily, giving Hob a hug. "Thank you!"

"Don't mention it," said Hob, blushing.

"Now we just need to find where Selena has hidden the locket!" said Aisha.

Emily frowned. "She said she was going to hide it in the darkest and most dangerous place in Enchanted Valley."

Hob scratched his head. "Well, that used to be the rocky cliffs around the cove. They were treacherous for ships, and steep and slippery to cross. But then the Starlight House was built, to make it light enough to see everything."

Emily gasped. "But the Starlight House isn't working any more."

"So the rocks around it are really dark again," said Silvermane. "And terribly dangerous for ships like Aurora's!"

"I bet that's where she's hidden the

locket!" said Aisha.

"You'd better find it, then," said Hob.
"Before it's too late for Aurora!"

Chapter Five
Lost in the Dark

Wind whipped against the girls' faces as
Silvermane swept through the night sky.
With the lantern they no longer needed
Flit to lead them, and he'd gratefully gone
back home to safety.

The ground below changed from grassy
fields to rocks and sand. The wind began

to blow harder, and the smell of the sea
filled the air.

"We must be getting close to the cliffs,"
said Aisha.

Just then, they soared out over a ridge of
rocks, and below them was the silvery sea.
Aisha lifted the lantern, shining its light
all around. There was the Starlight House,
not far away – a tall white tower on a
ragged cliff.

Emily caught sight of something

beyond it, glimmering out in the distance on the sea. "Are those ... sails?"

"It's Queen Aurora's ship!" gasped Silvermane. "Oh dear, we haven't a moment to lose. Without the light from the Starlight House, she'll sail straight on to the rocks!"

"Couldn't she fly to shore instead?" asked Aisha.

Silvermane shook her head. "She could, but there's a crew of sea sprites on board

her ship. Queen Aurora would never abandon them!"

"We could use Hob's lantern to signal to her," said Emily, thoughtfully.

"Great idea!" said Aisha.

Then a little voice came cheeping from the top of the dark cliffs. "Help! Oh please, won't someone help me?"

"Uh-oh!" said Emily. "Do you think someone's lost in the dark?"

"We'd better find out," said Silvermane. They flew lower, until the unicorn's hooves touched down on the cliff edge.

Scrambling off Silvermane's back, Emily and Aisha listened out for the cries.

"Help! I'm so terribly lost and alone!" the voice wailed.

"Over here!" said Emily. Aisha rushed to her side and they followed the cries and sad sniffs to a scrubby bush that sprouted from among the rocks. They looked at each other.

"I can't see anything," said Aisha.

"Move the lantern closer," said Emily.

Aisha bent down and held the lantern closer to the bush.

There was a nasty little snort of laughter. Then – *whooosh!* – a feathered creature burst out from its hiding place. Wings flapping wildly, it tore the lantern from Aisha's hands. She made a grab for it, but the bird was already rising into the sky.

"It's Screech!" cried Emily.

The light swung wildly, as the lantern dangled from the naughty owl's talons. "Tricked you again!" crowed Screech. "Now I've got your lantern! What are you going to do about that?"

Chapter Six
Broken!

"Get him!" cried Aisha. She dived forward, grasping at Screech with both hands …
But at the same moment Screech flapped and rose higher, just out of reach.

"Missed me!" jeered Screech. "Ha ha!"

"Leave him to me!" said Silvermane. With a lurch she took off, flying straight at the little owl.

Screech's big eyes went even wider.
But he darted across the cliffside to a big
tree that grew right on the edge. With a
rustle of leaves, he disappeared among the
branches, taking the light with him.

Silvermane slowed down and hovered
beside the tree. She poked her horn

through the leaves,
then shook her
head sadly. "The
branches are too
close together! I
can't get in …"

"Woo hoooo!"
hooted Screech,
from his hiding

place in the tree. "Silly unicorn! Silly girls!"

Emily came panting to a stop beside Aisha. They both looked up at the tree. "What's he going to do with our lantern?" wondered Emily.

There was another rustle of leaves. Then Screech's head popped out of the very top of the tree. He lifted the lantern in a talon. "It's my lantern now!" he called.

"Oh no it's not!" Aisha ran to the tree trunk. Gripping the rough bark with her fingertips, she began to climb. She pulled herself on to the lowest branch as quietly as possible. It swayed a little, but Screech was too busy gloating to notice.

"I'm going to smash the lantern!" said

Screech. "Then you won't be able to see! What do you think of that?"

Holding her breath, Aisha pulled herself up to a higher branch ... then another. She was almost at the top of the tree now. But as she stepped up on to the last branch, her foot slipped.

Craaack! A twig snapped.

Twit twoooo! Screech squawked in alarm. He turned his head right round, and spotted Aisha.

Aisha lunged for the lantern. Her hand closed over it, just as Screech tried to tug it away.

"Let go!" squealed Screech. He gave a yank with his talon, and the lantern flew through the air.

"No!" cried
Emily.

Down fell the
lantern, bumping
and bouncing
from branch
to branch …
then it dropped
straight off the edge of the
cliff. Aisha stared, pale with
shock.

Leaning from Silvermane's back, Emily
peered down the sheer cliff face. Far, far
below, she saw a twisted bit of metal
among the rocks. The bright orange liquid
seeped out of it, then turned dull and
disappeared.

"It's broken!" groaned Aisha.

Screech shot up into the sky in a flurry of feathers. "Let's see how you find that locket with no light!" he called back. Then he disappeared into the night, sniggering to himself.

"What should we do?" asked Aisha as she climbed back down through the branches. Emily, standing below, offered her a hand. Aisha took it, sliding carefully back to the ground. Now that darkness lay all around, she could hardly see a thing.

Silvermane landed beside the girls.

"There's only one thing we can do," said Silvermane. "We'll have to get the Starlight House working again.

Otherwise Queen Aurora's ship will hit the rocks! I really hope my locket is inside."

The unicorn was trembling, and Emily gently stroked her head. "Don't worry, Silvermane," she whispered. "We'll save Aurora … and we'll get your locket back too!"

Chapter Seven
The Starlight House

"I can almost see the Starlight House,"
said Aisha, peering into the darkness.
In the distance, the tall, pale shape of
the tower was visible. "I just can't see
anything else!"

Silvermane still looked worried, but she
stamped her hoof with determination.

"Hop on, girls," she said. "If we fly straight towards it, we should be all right."

A moment later they were soaring through the night. Emily and Aisha clung on tighter than ever. Now they had no stars to guide the way, no lantern and no Flit either. They couldn't see a thing but the ghostly tower up ahead ... and below, they could hear the waves crashing like thunder.

"I just hope we don't fall off," whispered

Emily, wrapping her arms firmly round Aisha's waist.

Suddenly Silvermane reared up, jolting the girls. "Whoa!" yelped Emily, clinging on tighter.

"Sorry!" said Silvermane, coming to a stop in the air. "I nearly flew straight into the Starlight House!"

"Don't worry," said Emily. "You did an amazing job flying us in the darkness."

"And at least we've arrived!" Aisha reached out and laid a hand on the pale surface. "It's the wall of the Starlight House," she said. "Phew!"

The girls trailed their hands over the white stones as Silvermane glided gently down. At last, the unicorn's hooves crunched in pebbles at the base of the Starlight House. "There!" cried Silvermane. She gave a whinny of relief. "Now we need to find the door. Lumi lives on the ground floor."

The girls slid off Silvermane's back and set off on foot, feeling their way around the base of the Starlight House with their hands on the walls.

"Lumi!" called Silvermane. "Are you in there?"

There was no reply.

"I hope Selena hasn't hurt him," said Emily anxiously.

"Ooh!" cried Aisha. "I've found something."

Emily joined her, and together they felt

the outline of a little wooden door. But it was hanging wide open.

"Lumi always keeps this door closed," Silvermane told the girls.

Aisha shivered. "I think someone else must have come to pay Lumi a visit," she whispered. Together they stepped inside, where it was even darker than it had been outside. The girls couldn't see a single thing.

Then they heard a strange, muffled squawking sound. "What is that?" asked Aisha.

"It sounds like Lumi!" said Silvermane, from the doorway.

The girls stepped further into the Starlight House. They went slowly and carefully, holding their arms out as far as they could.

"Ouch!" cried Aisha, as she banged into the arm of a sofa.

"Oops!" yelped Emily, knocking her shoulder against what felt like a lampshade.

"Mmmmff!" said the strange, muffled voice.

"I think I'm getting close," said Emily. She took another step, and her fingers brushed against something soft. "I feel … feathers!"

"That must be Lumi!" cried Aisha. She stumbled over. Together the girls felt the shape of a bird. But it was sitting on a chair, with ropes tied tightly around its body and beak.

As fast as they could, the girls found the knots and untied them.

When they got the bird's beak free, he gasped and shook his head. "Oh, thank you, girls!" he murmured, in a soft voice. "I am Lumi, and you must be Aisha and Emily. Now step back, please!"

As the girls edged away, Lumi hopped up on the chair. With a ruffling of feathers, he spread his wings. His feathers began to glow with a dim but golden light, and at last the girls

could see the Starlight House all around
them.

They were in a small, cosy living room
with orange walls and comfortable-
looking furniture all clustered around a
fireplace. A wooden spiral staircase led to
the floor above.

"What happened to you, Lumi?" asked
Aisha.

"It was that wicked Selena!" the

lightingale explained. "She broke down my door, burst in and tied me up …" As he spoke, his light flickered and went out. "I'm sorry," Lumi's voice came through the darkness. "I feel very weak now."

Silvermane stamped her hoof. "That wicked unicorn! How dare she?!"

Emily stroked Lumi's feathers. "Do you think Selena hid the locket in the Starlight House?"

"I don't think so," said Lumi, shaking his head. "She didn't stay for long."

Aisha groaned. "It's a dead end!" she said. Then she froze, staring out of the window. "Hang on … Do you see that?"

Out in the darkness, something was gleaming with a faint, silvery light.

Looking closer, Emily saw that the glow came from the jagged rocks at the edge of the cliff. "Do you think ..." she breathed. "Could it be the locket? The edge of the cliff is probably the most dangerous place in the whole kingdom."

Twit twooooo! Beyond the window, a little creature came diving out of the night, heading straight for the glinting silver light.

Screech!

Hearts racing, Emily and Aisha dashed through the doorway. Silvermane was already galloping toward the cliff edge. "Go away, Screech!" cried the unicorn. "Shoo!"

"Shoo yourself!" squawked Screech.

He stretched out his wings as he soared towards the rocks …

Then Lumi hopped up on the window ledge. He lunged forward and made a grab for Screech.

With a squeal of surprise, Screech jerked away. "Urgh!" he yelped. "Where did you come from? I thought we'd tied you up!"

Screech fell to the ground. Silvermane reached forward and pinned Screech's tail feathers under her hoof, just as Lumi's light faded to a thin glow. The lightingale was panting from the effort.

"Hurry, girls!" Silvermane called. "You get the locket!"

Emily and Aisha ran to the jagged rocks where they'd seen the silver light. In the dim glow from Lumi's wings, they could finally see the locket clearly. It was dangling by its chain from a sharp bit of rock at the very edge of the cliff. Below, they could just make out the waves crashing against huge, jagged rocks on the shore. And beyond, Aurora's ship was coming, sailing straight into danger …

Holding hands, the girls stepped carefully across the rough and bumpy rocks, going as fast as they dared. As they

came closer to the edge they

staying low so they wouldn't fa

"I think I can get it," said Aisha,

brow creased with concentration. "Just

hold on to me …"

Emily knelt and held on to Aisha's top.

Then Aisha crawled forward, reaching as

far as she could with her right hand. Her

fingers brushed at the locket.

She flinched, trying to ignore the

terrifying drop just ahead of her, and the

churning of the sea far below …

"Just a little further," Aisha muttered.

She stretched as far as she could, until …

Yes! She hooked a finger round the chain

and flicked it free.

At once, Emily pulled Aisha back from

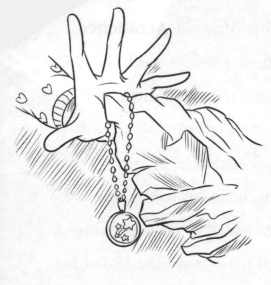

the edge.

Aisha gripped the locket tightly in her hand, so there was no chance of it slipping away. "Come on!"

Emily gasped. "We have to save Aurora's ship!" The silver-sailed vessel was leaping over the waves … heading straight for the rocks.

The girls scrambled back from the cliff edge, towards the Starlight House. Screech was still trying to pull his tail out from under Silvermane's hoof.

Aisha broke into a sprint. As she reached Silvermane, the unicorn lowered her head, and Aisha draped the locket around her neck.

At once the locket shone, bright silver. A shimmer of sparkles ran across Silvermane's coat, and her horn glittered with a magical light. Silvermane let out a long, happy sigh and flicked her tail with joy. "Thank you, girls!"

"Noooo!" wailed Screech as he wriggled free.

Emily and Aisha gasped as they looked

up at the sky. The stars were coming out again, winking like fairy lights.

"You did it!" cried Lumi, dancing from talon to talon and shaking his golden feathers, which were bursting with bright golden light.

The girls looked at each other and grinned.

"Oops – I almost forgot … there's no time to lose!" cried Lumi. The lightingale swept up into the air, beating his golden wings and ducking through a window at the top of the Starlight House. A moment later, a white beam of light shone from the top of the Starlight House, making the ocean glint like a thousand diamonds.

"I can't see," said Silvermane, peering

towards the ocean. "Is the ship turning?"

Emily and Aisha looked at each other again. But this time, their faces were full of worry. *Oh no … did we make it in time to save Aurora?*

Chapter Eight
Aurora Returns

The girls held their breath.

They could see the waves crashing against the jagged black rocks now, far below, and Queen Aurora's ship was sailing straight towards them. The silver sails were smooth and full as the ship cut through the water ...

"No!" gasped Emily.

Then Aisha gripped Emily's hand tight. The sails were turning. And the ship was too! It curved away, just missing the closest of the rocks, and steered towards Shimmer Bay.

"Phew!" The girls let out their breath in a sigh of relief.

"We did it!" cried Silvermane, rearing up joyfully.

"Curses!" howled Screech. The little owl twitched his wings and flapped furiously away. A moment later he had disappeared around the edge of the cliff.

Lumi came gliding down from the Starlight House to land beside the girls. He spread his wings around them. His

feathers were
warm and soft,
and the girls
hugged him
tightly. "Thank
you, Emily
and Aisha!"

murmured Lumi. "You saved the stars!
Now I can light the way for every ship
that comes to visit Enchanted Valley."

"Thank you," said Aisha. "We couldn't
have got the locket back without you."

"Or saved Queen Aurora's ship!" added
Emily.

"Come on, let's go and welcome her
back," said Silvermane.

Lumi waved with the tip of a golden

wing, as they climbed on to Silvermane's back once again. Then with a flick of her tail, Silvermane was swooping through the sky above the cliffside, towards Shimmer Bay. With the stars twinkling overhead, they could see the whole valley laid out below, like a beautiful map made of silver.

The girls couldn't stop grinning the whole way.

At one end of Shimmer Bay there was a long wooden pier, painted white. As Silvermane flew down low, the girls saw that Aurora's ship had just reached the pier. A gangplank was lowered on to it, like a drawbridge. Then a familiar unicorn came trotting off the ship. She

was glowing with a pinkish-red colour,
like a sunset, and her crown glittered gold.

Queen Aurora!

Silvermane landed with a gentle thunk
of her hooves on the wooden pier. The
girls slid off her back, then rushed to
Queen Aurora and buried their faces in
her soft coat.

"You came!" said Queen Aurora.

"And they saved Enchanted Valley

again!" Silvermane told her.

"You are clever girls," Queen Aurora said, nuzzling them.

"We weren't going to let Selena win," said Emily. "But we couldn't have done it alone."

"It's like Flit's song said," added Aisha. "*We've got our friends and that's all we need. Selena won't win, she'll never succeed.*"

Aurora whinnied in delight. "What a fabulous song!"

Behind her, the crew of sea sprites had begun tying up the ship and taking down the sails. They were little blue-green creatures with pointed ears and shaggy seaweed hair, and they scampered around

the deck like
monkeys.

"We're just glad
to see that you're
all right," said
Aisha. "We were
worried about you!"

Queen Aurora nodded gravely. "When
I got that message, I thought I'd find
someone in trouble. But instead, when
I got to the island there was just a big
black scorch mark in the sand … shaped
like a lightning bolt!"

"Selena!" said Emily.

"That's right." Queen Aurora sighed.
"I guessed she was up to something. And
that's when I summoned you girls."

"We're so glad you did," said Aisha.

"We'll always be ready to help the unicorns," added Emily.

Queen Aurora led them down the pier and on to the beach. All the little animals, pixies and elves had gathered around the three remaining Night Sparkle Unicorns. Huddled together, they all had their heads tipped back, as they stared at a sky bright with stars. Their eyes shone with wonder, and with happiness too.

Just then, the sky lit up with a burst of white light. *BOOOOM!* Thunder rolled in the distance.

The girls' hearts sank. *Uh-oh ... Selena!*

Sure enough, the silver unicorn flew out from behind a cloud. She hovered in mid-

air, and Screech came flapping after her, scowling at the girls.

Selena snorted crossly. "I suppose you think you're clever?" she called. "Well, you might have got the Star Locket back … but I still have the other three! This night will go on for ever, until I'm queen. And I'll make sure it's the most miserable night ever!"

Selena threw back her head and cackled, and Screech hooted along with her. There was another flash of lightning, and a rumble of thunder. Then Selena and Screech surged up into the sky and vanished in the darkness.

"She really is wicked," said Dreamspell, hanging her head.

"She'll never give us our lockets back," added Slumbertail sadly.

Emily and Aisha ran across the sand and hugged each Night Sparkle Unicorn in turn.

"Don't worry," said Aisha when they'd finished. "We'll get your lockets back. We promise!"

"We'll stop Selena," said Emily. "Together!"

"Yes, we will," said Silvermane. "But first, how about some hot chocolate?"

"Yes, please," said Emily and Aisha together, giggling.

The girls opened Dreamspell's silver saddlebag, took out a fluffy white blanket and spread it on the sand. Then they

passed round a purple thermos full of
hot chocolate, as they settled down on
the blanket. The drink was warm, sweet
and delicious. Emily and Aisha lay back
happily to gaze at the night sky, as
Silvermane pointed out constellations
with her glowing horn.

"There's the Pufflebunny," Silvermane
was saying, as the girls looked at a
pattern of stars shaped like rabbit ears.

"And there's the Teddy Bear!" She pointed at another little cluster of stars.

Queen Aurora yawned. "Speaking of teddy bears … I'm exhausted after that journey! I think it's time for bed."

Emily and Aisha couldn't help yawning too.

"We'd better head home," said Aisha a little sadly. "But what about the other lockets?"

"We'll see you again very soon, and we'll find the lockets then," said Queen Aurora. "But you girls need your rest."

Emily and Aisha hugged Queen Aurora. Then they ran to Silvermane and threw their arms around the unicorn.

"Thank you, girls," whispered

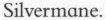

Silvermane.

At last it was time to go. Queen Aurora waved her horn like a magic wand, and a cloud of golden sparkles shimmered in the air. They swirled around the girls like a gust of snowflakes, faster and faster, brighter and brighter, until the girls could see nothing but golden light. And slowly, their feet lifted off the ground …

As the light faded, Emily and Aisha found themselves standing in the dark garden at

Enchanted Cottage. The night was calm and silent, and their tartan blanket was still spread out on the grass. Everything was just as it had been when they left.

Emily glanced up and felt a rush of relief to see that the sky was studded with stars.

"It's just as beautiful as the night sky in Enchanted Valley," sighed Aisha. "Well … almost!"

Then both girls gasped. Something had swished across the sky. A streak of gold, trailing glitter behind it.

"Was that a shooting star?" breathed Emily.

"It looked more like Lumi the Lightingale!" said Aisha.

The girls turned to each other in amazement, and grinned.

"When do you think Queen Aurora will call us back?" wondered Aisha.

"I don't know," said Emily. "But I can't wait!"

The End

Join Emily and Aisha
for another adventure in ...
Dreamspell's Special Wish
Read on for a sneak peek!

In her cosy bedroom, Aisha Khan and
her best friend, Emily Turner, were getting
ready for bed. Bright moonlight shone
through the small window under the thick
thatched roof of Enchanted Cottage,
and faraway stars twinkled like magic
lanterns.

"Today was so fun," Aisha sighed
happily. "I still can't believe you get to
stay for the whole week!"

"Me neither!" said Emily. "School
holidays are the best. What shall we do
tomorrow?"

"Hmmm," Aisha said. "You showed me how to make that brilliant baking soda volcano today, so tomorrow, maybe I could teach you how to play badminton?"

"Sounds great!" laughed Emily.

Read
Dreamspell's Special Wish
to find out what adventures are in store for Aisha and Emily!

Also available

Book Five:

Silvermane Saves the Stars

Book Six:

Dreamspell's Special Wish

Book Seven:

Slumbertail & the Sleep Pixies

Book Eight:

Brighteye & the Blue Moon

Unicorn Magic

Look out for the next book!

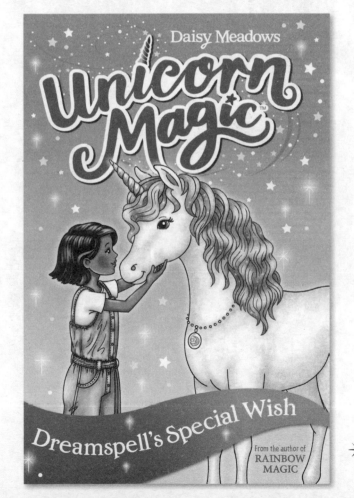

Daisy Meadows

Unicorn Magic™

Dreamspell's Special Wish

From the author of
RAINBOW
MAGIC

If you like
Unicorn Magic,
you'll love ...

Welcome to Animal Ark!

Animal-mad Amelia is sad
about moving house, until she
discovers Animal Ark, where vets look
after all kinds of animals in need.

Join Amelia and her friend Sam for a
brand-new series of animal adventures!